BAD MOON

Dudley Bromley

A Pacemaker® Book

Globe Fearon

Upper Saddle River,
New Jersey

The PACEMAKER BESTELLERS

Bestellers I

Diamonds in the Dirt
Night of the Kachina
The Verlaine Crossing
Silvabamba
The Money Game
Flight to Fear
The Time Trap
The Candy Man
Three Mile House
Dream of the Dead

Bestellers II

Black Beach
Crash Dive
Wind Over Stonehenge
Gypsy
Escape from Tomorrow
The Demeter Star
North to Oak Island
So Wild a Dream
Wet Fire
Tiger, Lion, Hawk

Bestellers III

Star Gold
Bad Moon
Jungle Jenny
Secret Spy
Little Big Top
The Animals
Counterfeit!
Night of Fire and Blood
Village of Vampires
I Died Here

Bestellers IV

Dares
Welcome to Skull Canyon
Blackbeard's Medal
Time's Reach
Trouble at Catskill Creek
The Cardiff Hill Mystery
Tomorrow's Child
Hong Kong Heat
Follow the Whales
A Changed Man

Series director: Rober G. Bander
Designer: Richard Kharibian
Cover designer and illustrator: John Lytle

ISBN: 0-8224-5362-2

Library of Congress Catalog Card Number: 78-72330
Printed in the United States of America.
5 6 7 8 9 10 04 03 02 01 00

CONTENTS

CHAPTER 1
NO-NAME

Karl Baumer's watch had stopped.

The watch said 3:15, but Karl knew it was much later than that. For one thing, he could see the sky from his office window. The sky was already growing dark.

Probably past six, Karl thought.

He wasn't surprised that his watch had stopped. It had been that kind of day. He had dropped his breakfast eggs that morning–right on the floor. Then his car wouldn't start. Then the bus he took to his office bumped into a fire truck. Then he broke his key opening his office door.

It had *not* been a good day.

But Karl Baumer, private detective, knew the reason why.

Karl had seen many days like this one. And *he blamed them all on the moon.* When silly things happened all day long, he knew it was because of what he called a Bad Moon.

"There's going to be a Bad Moon out tonight," he would say. He said those very words soon after he broke his key that morning. "There's going to be a Bad Moon out tonight," he said.

And he was right.

Karl Baumer got up from behind his desk and walked over to the only window in his office. He looked down on *Berlinerstrasse*, the main street in Frankfurt, West Germany. As always, the street was busy with people.

Karl was waiting. Most days, he left his office before dark. But today he knew he had to wait. He knew that every Bad Moon brought at least one very strange case to his door. It was sure to happen. Someone would show up with a problem—a strange problem. No Bad Moon had ever passed without at least one.

"Mr. Baumer?"

Karl jumped. He had not heard anyone come into his office. But someone had. Karl turned around and saw a short man standing next to him. Karl looked at the door to his office. It was closed. He wondered how the short man had been able to come in and close the door without making a sound.

The short man looked about 45. He had on a long coat and a hat. He stood very still, waiting for Karl to speak.

Karl knew that the short man was the person he had been waiting for.

"Yes, I'm Karl Baumer. Who are you?"

"Call me No-Name."

"Why? Don't you have a name?"

"Just call me No-Name."

"OK, OK. What can I do for you, No-Name?"

"Have you ever heard of a magician by the name of Merl the Magnificent?"

"Of course," said Karl. "He was one of the best magicians who ever lived. He killed himself about ten years ago–right?"

"He died 13 years ago tonight."

No-Name moved very close to Karl. He spoke slowly. "And Merl did not kill himself, Mr. Baumer. He was murdered."

"But all the papers said–"

"I don't care what the papers said. There were five people with Merl the night he died. One of them killed Merl."

"Have you talked to the police about this?"

"More than once, believe me. But they seem to think that Merl killed himself. To them, the case is closed. But not to me."

"Why don't you think Merl killed himself?"

"I just don't, that's all. That's why I need your help, Mr. Baumer. I want to know what you think."

No-Name handed Karl a piece of paper. He also gave him four 1,000 mark notes.

"Here's some money ahead of time. And the address of Merl's house is written on this

paper," No-Name told Karl. "Be there around 8:30 tonight. The five of us should be there by then."

"Us?" asked Karl. "You mean–you're one of the five people?"

"Yes," said No-Name. "I am. The five of us meet every year at Merl's house on the day of his death."

Karl couldn't believe his ears. "Why on earth do you do that? I don't understand."

"You will, Mr. Baumer. You will."

Karl looked at the address. It was near the *Tiergarten*, the Frankfurt zoo. It wouldn't be hard to find. "OK, No-Name. I'll be there."

"Good," said the little man.

Karl turned to his desk and opened a drawer. "I'll need you to fill out these papers first," he said. But when he turned around again, No-Name was gone. Once again the man had opened and closed the door without a sound.

Karl put the papers down. He wondered what the night would bring. If No-Name was a sample of what was to come, it didn't look good. He walked over to the window and looked out. The moon had just come up.

There it is, he thought. It's a Bad Moon, all right. A full moon, like always.

Then he shook his head. He had never seen a Bad Moon that looked so red before.

CHAPTER 2

The Great Escape

Karl Baumer had a good friend who worked at the *Frankfurter Chronik*. The man's name was Hans, and he was over 70 years old. Hans' job was to keep the old newspaper files in order. When someone needed to know about something that had happened in the past, they went to Hans. Hans had filed and recorded almost every news story the *Chronik* printed since he went to work there more than 50 years ago.

Karl had gone to see Hans as soon as No-Name had left his office.

"Sure, I remember that one," Hans told Karl. He looked through a big file drawer in his giant office. "He killed himself–right?"

"So they've been saying for the past 13 years. But maybe not."

Hans looked up, and his eyes grew big. "You think he was–murdered?"

"Just find the file, Hans."

"I'm looking," said the old man as he turned back to the drawer. "I know I have a big file on Merl the Magnificent. He was very famous, you know. It should be right here. Yes, here it is."

Karl sat down and opened the file. It was filled with papers. The papers went all the way back to 1938—the year of Merl's first big escape trick. Story after story in the file told about Merl's other escapes. Next to Houdini, Merl was the most famous magician in European history.

Merl's real name had been Harry Wong. He had changed his name soon after he went into show business. He had named himself after Merlin, a famous magician. Merlin had lived at the same time as King Arthur.

One story said that Merl had killed himself—just two days before he was to stage something called the Great Escape. Merl had said again and again that the Great Escape would make him more famous than Houdini and Merlin put together. But Merl had kept all the facts about the Great Escape to himself. No one knew what Merl had been planning to do for his great trick.

Another story in the file was about the five people who were in Merl's house the night he died. Karl read that story with much interest. All five of the people told the police that Merl had talked a lot about "returning from the dead." One of the people said, "Merl kept telling us he could escape from anything—even death. Perhaps he killed himself to show the world he could really do it. Perhaps this is the Great Escape that he has been talking about."

Still another news story—written much later—told about Merl's house. The house was supposed to be haunted. Nobody knew *how* it was haunted. But everyone stayed away.

Karl came to the last story in the file. It was another story about the five people. This story backed up what No-Name had told Karl. It said that the five people who were in Merl's house the night he died went back there every year. It said they were meeting to see if Merl would ever return from the dead—as he had said he would. The story also said that the five people never talked about their nights in the house. All they ever said was that they had not yet seen or heard from Merl's ghost.

"Karl. You're still here."

Hans was standing by the door. His eyes were red, and he rubbed them.

Karl closed the file. "What time is it, Hans?" he asked his friend.

"It's close to eight," said the old man.

Karl jumped up. He thanked Hans and ran down the stairs to the street. He rushed into Rhinetour Rent-a-Car, which was next door to the *Chronik*. Because it was Friday night, Rhinetour had only one car left to rent. Karl didn't want the car, but he had to take it. He didn't want to be late for *this* meeting.

Five minutes later, he drove an orange Volkswagen bus out of Rhinetour's lot. He shook his arm at the Bad Moon. He hated the way it was looking down on him. It seemed like a giant eye in the night sky.

CHAPTER **3**

CRAZY PETRA

Karl stopped the car.

He checked the address again, just to be sure. Then he parked the car on the street and got out. The wind had been blowing, but it stopped as he closed the car door. Now the air was very still.

Karl stood beside the car for a long time, looking up at the house before him. The house was very old and very big. It sat up against the side of a hill. It had many big windows and a tall door made of wood. And it was very dark. Karl could see no lights on inside the house.

No one home, Karl thought. I wonder if the party has been called off?

He checked the address again. More than once in his life he had gone to the wrong address. But not this time. This was the right house, all right. This was the house where Merl the Magnificent had died—13 years ago to the day.

Lightning!

The flash was sudden and bright. It made Karl jump. The lightning itself lasted only a second. But the loud crack that followed it was long and slow and shook the ground. After it was over, Karl looked up. The sky was growing dark. The wind was picking up again. A storm was on the way.

Karl decided to try the door of the house. If he could get inside, he would build a fire. That way the place would be warm when the others got there. And he would stay dry if the rain started.

He started down the long walk toward the front door. A giant old tree stood beside the walk. The tree was dead and broken. It seemed to be reaching out, trying to stop Karl from going up to the house. As he walked past the tree, Karl felt very strange.

Lightning!

During the flash, Karl could see that the big door to the house was wide open. He was sure that the door had been closed when he first looked at the house. He wondered if someone was playing a trick on him.

"Hello," Karl called out, as he neared the door. "Is anyone there?"

"Hello," came a voice from inside the house. It sounded like someone shouting from the bottom of a deep well. "Is that you, No-Name?"

"No," said Karl. "My name is Baumer. Karl Baumer. Can I come in? It looks like rain."

The voice shouted back at him. "Well, are you going to come in or not?"

Karl climbed the steps and walked into the house. As soon as he closed the door behind him, it began to rain outside.

Lightning!

For just a second, the house was as bright as day. Karl saw that he was standing in a long hall. He also saw Petra. She looked like she was 200 years old. She had eyes like a wild animal, and crazy red hair that stuck out all over her head.

Karl felt very strange. When that lightning was over, he couldn't see anything again. "Can we turn on a light or something?" he asked Petra.

Petra laughed at Karl's question. "You fool," she said. Then she walked off down the dark hall.

Karl stood in the hall, trying to decide if he should follow Petra. Then, he heard her open and close a door at the other end of the hall. After that, everything was quiet in the house. The only sound was the rain falling outside.

Karl had almost decided to follow the old woman when some strange things happened. First a loud horn went off. Then a red light flashed, and the floor moved up and down. Then a bell rang. Then the lights came on. After that, everything was quiet again.

What was going on?

Karl stood there for a moment, thinking so hard it made his head hurt. He decided to follow Petra right away. It was either that or go crazy trying to decide if he had gone crazy or not.

He made his way down the hall and soon came to a door. Without waiting even a second, he opened it.

CHAPTER 4

HOUSE OF TRICKS

The door opened into a giant room—a study. Several lights were on. And a big fire was burning in the fireplace. Four people sat around the fire—Petra and three others.

These are the same people who were in this house the night Merl the Magnificent died, Karl thought. Only No-Name is missing.

Karl walked into the study. He took a few steps toward the people and then stopped. He looked at the people, and they looked back at him. No one said anything for what seemed like a long time. Finally, one of the people—a very well-dressed man—stood up.

"Welcome," said the man, "to the House of Tricks."

Lightning!

"The House of Tricks?" said Karl. "You

mean, something really did happen in the hall just now?"

The man smiled. "Yes," he said. "Merl loved that one. He loved this house, too. He built it himself, you know. From his own plans. At one time there must have been more than 100 different tricks built into this house. Just waiting to jump out at you from all over."

"At one time?" asked Karl.

"That's right," said the man. His smile did not change or move when he talked. Karl thought the smile seemed painted on the man's face.

The man went on. "We've had all of the tricks taken out over the years—except for the hall. The hall is always good for a laugh. It was Merl's favorite, too."

The trick hall explains a lot, thought Karl. It explains how some people might think the house is haunted, without ever seeing a ghost.

Karl noticed everyone looking at him. It seemed to be his turn to talk. "Merl sounds like he was a lot of fun," he said.

"That he was, Mr. Baumer," said the man with the smile.

"You know my name?"

"Petra told us."

Karl looked at Petra. She was looking right at him. She smiled. She didn't have any teeth.

The black hole that was Petra's mouth made Karl think of something that had been on his mind.

"Why does this house look so dark from the outside?" he asked. "Were you people in here a while ago with all the lights turned out—or what?"

"No, of course not," the man said, without breaking his smile. "The power has been going off and on for some time now. I suppose it's the storm that's doing it. So when you first saw the house, the power must have been off."

And it just happened to come back on while I was all alone in the hall, Karl thought. He didn't believe that for a minute.

"By the way," said the man with the smile. "My name is Franco Pantela. You may have heard of me. I work under the name of The Great Wizzo."

Then Karl broke into a smile of his own. "I have heard of you," he said. "I've seen you on TV a lot. You're a famous magician."

Franco seemed very pleased with himself. "Yes, I am," he said. "But only because I had a very good teacher. Everything I know about magic I learned from Merl the Magnificent."

As he spoke, Franco moved his arms in the air. Suddenly, he was holding an egg in one of his hands. Then two eggs. Then three.

"Oh, knock it off, Franco," said the other man in the room. He was tall and thin with thick glasses. He stood up and faced Karl. "A magician is never offstage, Mr. Baumer," the man said.

"Who are you?" Karl wanted to know.

"My name is Mark Steiner. I worked for Merl. I did his bookkeeping."

"I see," said Karl. Then he turned to the one person in the room he hadn't met. She had deep blue eyes and long yellow hair. Karl thought that the woman looked as smart as she did beautiful.

"What's your name?" he asked her.

The woman turned her head slowly and looked up at Karl. When she spoke, her voice sounded cold and stiff.

"Lola Nikel," she said. Then she turned her head away and looked at the fire.

"Did you know Merl?"

It was a very long time before Lola Nikel said anything. And when she finally did, it was not in answer to Karl's question.

"I don't believe you've told us anything about yourself, Mr. Baumer," she said. "Just what are you doing here tonight?"

Karl smiled at Lola. "You look as if you belong on the stage," he said. He was killing time, thinking. Karl wasn't sure what he should tell these people. He looked over at the two men, Franco and Mark. They seemed to be waiting for him to say something.

Then Petra started laughing like a wild woman. "We haven't got all night, you fool," she said.

CHAPTER 5

The Night Merl Died

"I'm a private detective," said Karl.

As he spoke, Karl looked around at the people in the room. It was always interesting to see that look in people's eyes when he told them he was a private detective. It was often a good way to find out if a person had anything to hide.

"A private eye," said Franco. His smile was gone now. "What are you doing here? Who sent you?"

Karl thought it best not to tell them about No-Name's visit to his office—at least not right away. "I've always been interested in this case," he said.

"Case?" said Franco. "What case? Merl killed himself—or haven't you heard?"

"I've heard. But I haven't believed. You know what I mean?"

"No."

"Well, it seems to me that Merl really enjoyed life. He had a good time while he was alive. Why would a man like that kill himself? I just don't understand it."

No one seemed to have an answer to Karl's question. After a minute, Mark walked across the room to a bar near the study door. He began fixing himself a drink. Then he asked if anyone else wanted anything. No one did.

Mark took his time. When he finished, he took a long drink from his glass. Then he turned to Karl. "Do you really think Merl was murdered, Mr. Baumer?"

"I haven't decided–yet."

"But that is why you were sent here, isn't it–to find out if Merl was murdered?"

"I'll just say this, Mr. Steiner. If Merl *was* murdered, I'll soon know how it was done and who did it."

As he spoke, Karl looked once again from person to person. It's no use, he thought. They all look guilty.

Franco Pantela, the magician, moved next to the fire. "You realize, I hope, that one of us is not here yet."

Karl knew that No-Name was missing, but

he acted like he didn't know. "Oh?" he said. "Who?"

Petra was laughing again. "You fool, you fool, you fool."

Karl felt strange every time Petra called him a fool. But none of the others seemed to notice the old woman, or what she said.

Franco went on. "He calls himself No-Name," he said. "That is all we know about him. In all the time we've spent with No-Name, he's never told us anything about himself—nothing."

Karl could believe that without any trouble. "Was No-Name a good friend of Merl's?" he asked.

Now Mark spoke up again. "Most of the time," he said, "Merl and No-Name played jokes and carried on together like little kids. But the night Merl died, the two of them were fighting about something. We never did find out what their fight was about."

Karl was very interested in Mark's story. He wanted to hear more about what happened that night. "There's a lot I don't know about the night Merl died," he said. "Would you mind filling me in?"

Mark looked around at the others in the room. No one said anything. Finally, Mark finished his drink and started toward the bar again.

"It was Saturday," he said, as he reached the bar. "It was really raining outside—like it is now. The storm was so bad that Merl had us all spend the night. And all night he wanted to talk about life after death. He wanted to know what the five of us thought about it. Most of all, he wanted to know if we believed in ghosts. I'm afraid we made fun of a lot of what Merl said. We laughed at him when he said he would come back to earth after he died. He became very angry. He went up to his room, and that was the last time we saw him alive."

Lightning!

"We waited down here in the study for half an hour or so. I'd say we each went up at least once to knock on Merl's door—to try to get him to come back down. But he never said anything to any of us. We finally gave up and went to our rooms. That's when we heard the gun go off. We all ran out into the hall—everyone but Merl, that is. We rushed into his room. I was the first one to see him. I'll never forget it as long as I live."

Karl could think of a lot of questions to ask about that night 13 years ago. But they would all have to wait.

A sudden crashing sound came from one of the rooms on the second floor of the house. The sound was followed by other strange noises.

Petra started to yell. "It's Merl!" she said. "He's come back! He's come back!"

CHAPTER 6

Secrets of Magic

Karl was the first one out of the study. Like everyone else, he was headed for the stairs. But he forgot about the trick hall. He stopped dead in his tracks when the horn sounded and the red light flashed. And he almost fell over when the floor moved up and down and the bell rang. The whole thing was more of a surprise this time than it had been the first time.

Before Karl began to move again, everyone —even Petra—had passed him. When he finally reached the top of the stairs, everyone was standing by an open door at one end of the hall. They were all looking through the door opening into a room. And they seemed to be surprised by what they saw.

"This was Merl's room," said Franco as Karl moved in to have a look. Karl saw that a desk and a table had been turned over in the large room. It looked like the bed had also been moved. And a big case full of props from Merl's magic acts had been knocked over.

"Strange," said Mark. "Why would anyone come in here just to mess things up?"

"Does anyone know," asked Karl, "if anything like this has ever happened before?"

"I don't think it has," said Franco.

"No," said Lola Nikel, "never."

"It's Merl, I tell you," Petra said. Her eyes moved from side to side, and she walked in a big circle around the room. "Merl's ghost is going to be here for sure. Merl! Merl, can you hear me? Can you see me, Merl?"

Mark reached out and took Petra's hand. But he spoke to the others. "I'll take Petra back down to the study," he said. Then he turned to the old woman. "Come on, Petra."

Petra and Mark went out the door as Franco and Karl began to put the room back in order. They moved the bed and fixed the table and desk. As they worked, Franco explained about Petra.

"She's always been a little crazy," he said. "But it does seem to be worse than ever this year." He shook his head, then went on. "Merl loved her like a mother. She gave him his very first job as a magician—got him started in show business."

Karl saw Lola trying to pick up the prop case. He turned away from Franco to help her lift it.

Then he began helping Lola put the props back in the case.

"You worked with Merl on stage, didn't you?" he asked Lola. He tried to sound as nice as possible.

"That's right," she said. To Karl's surprise, she didn't seem to mind the question. As a matter of fact, she went on talking. "Merl and I were a great team. I could almost read his mind, you know. It gave our act a special touch of magic–the timing was always perfect."

There seemed to be a large number of props to pick up. Karl found them all very interesting. He had seen magician's props like these in the past, but not up close. Things like metal rings, top hats, playing cards. But Karl also found several kinds of props that most magicians never used. Things like guns, heavy rope, and iron locks of all shapes and sizes.

Then Karl remembered something. "You know, I saw Merl once–about 15 years ago at the Imperial Theater in Berlin. Were you with him then?"

"Of course."

"I'll never forget that show. I should have remembered you. But, you know, I was watching the act, not your faces. You both were great."

"Thank you, Mr. Baumer."

"Call me Karl."

"Karl, did you know that a magician's assistant is really the one doing most of the tricks in an act? About all the magician ever does is keep the people looking right at him or her. While that's happening, the assistant pulls off the tricks. Next time you see a magic act, watch the assistant, not the magician."

"That's very interesting," said Karl. He was looking at the many different kinds of guns in Merl's case. "What were all the guns used for?"

"There were several tricks—like the one where I stood in front of a glass door. Then Merl pointed a gun at me and fired. I wasn't hurt, but the glass door broke into a million pieces."

"How in the world. . . ."

"A trick door, of course. We never used live shells in our guns—only blanks."

"I see."

By this time, Franco had finished with his part of the cleanup. He came over and joined Karl and Lola by the prop case. "There was also the two-gun trick," he said. "That one was my idea. I still use it, as a matter of fact."

Suddenly Lola looked like she was upset. "I think I'll go see how Petra is doing," she said. And then she walked out of the room.

Karl thought about following her. But he didn't. He wasn't really ready to leave the room yet. He moved toward the bed, pointing. "Is that where Merl's body was found?" he asked Franco.

"Yes. You can still see his blood there on the rug. It never came out."

Karl looked at the blood. It was a large black spot on the rug by the bed. "Do you think Merl's ghost will ever show up?" he asked Franco suddenly.

Franco didn't wait even a second to answer. "No," he said. "But that's made me remember something. When Mark was telling you about the night Merl died—remember?"

"Yes."

"Well, he left out the most important part."

Lightning!

CHAPTER 7

HAUNTED TELEVISION

Karl sat down on the bed, right next to where Merl's body had been found 13 years before. Karl was very interested in what Franco had to say.

"No one was ever supposed to know this," the magician said. "Merl asked us never to tell anyone. But I don't see how you can ever solve this case if you don't know."

Franco walked over to the door and pushed it closed. "So they won't hear me tell you," he explained. Then he walked over to the bed and sat down. He spoke in a whisper.

"More than anything in the world, Merl wanted to prove to us that he could return from the dead. He said that if anyone could do it, he could. And he said that if it were really possible—if ghosts were real, in other words—then he would come back after he died. He even came up with a way to prove it."

Lightning!

"How can you prove something like that?" Karl wanted to know.

"Merl gave us each a number. I'm 43-left. Lola is 19-right. And so on. All the numbers in the right order will open a safe down in the study. But one number—the first number—is missing. That number belongs to Merl. He didn't tell us that one. His ghost is supposed to let us know what the number is. Only then can we open the safe and divide what's inside."

"And what is inside?"

"One million dollars."

Karl shook his head slowly. "A million dollars! And Merl didn't tell all of you about this until the night he died?"

"That's right—just before he got angry with us and came up here to his room. But he must have been planning it for some time. It was all set down in his will. And he had had Mark get the money out of his bank—the day before he died. Mark even saw him put the money in the safe."

Karl sat for a while without saying anything. He was thinking, trying to fit the different pieces together. But he finally gave up. It's too soon, he thought. There are still too many missing pieces.

"Thanks," Karl said as he stood up. "What you've told me will help." Then he turned to the door.

"I hope so," said Franco, getting up off the bed. "Merl was my best friend, Mr. Baumer."

But Karl wasn't listening. He had already walked out of the room and into the second floor hall. Franco came right behind him.

Karl saw a door right across the hall from Merl's room. And at the other end of the hall, there were four more doors. Two were on each side.

"Six rooms?" Karl asked Franco.

"Yes. Six up here and four on the first floor."

"Are there doors between any of the rooms up here?"

Franco shook his head. "No. Each room has only one door—the one that opens into the hall."

"Hmm," said Karl. Then he started for the stairs, and Franco followed close behind. They were halfway down the stairs when they had to stop. All the lights in the house went out.

"The storm must have knocked the power out again," said Franco.

Once their eyes were used to the dark, Karl and Franco finished their trip down to the study. The trick hall didn't work this time—there was no power to make it work.

But as soon as Karl walked into the study, he forgot all about the trick hall. Karl stopped suddenly, and so did Franco. Like everyone else in the room, they were looking at a very strange sight.

In a corner of the study was a big old television set—and it was on! Its picture made a bright light when every other light in the house was dark. But the picture itself was most frightening of all.

It was Merl the Magnificent!

Lightning!

LIGHTNING!

For several seconds, everyone in the room looked at the television. The picture of Merl didn't move or talk. It just looked out from its TV window, like it was studying the room and the people in it.

Karl was about to take a close look at the haunted television. But he never made it. The television went out. And then someone screamed.

Karl thought it was Lola Nikel who

screamed, but he wasn't sure. And he never got the chance to find out.

Something crashed against him and knocked him to the floor. The thing—whatever it was—was heavy and covered with mud. It fell right on top of Karl and lay on him like a dead fish.

Karl's heart was pounding. He tried to get free, but he couldn't. He was trapped.

Then the lights came on. Karl saw Mark and Franco. They were standing over him, looking down. They reached down and lifted the wet thing off him.

Only then did Karl realize that the thing was a living man.

No-Name!

CHAPTER 8

Too Many Reasons

At first, No-Name could not talk.

Karl, Franco, and Mark helped him over to sit by the fire. Then Lola covered him with a dry coat, and Mark made him a drink.

Petra stood by herself in the center of the room, watching everything.

"My car was washed off the road by a wall of mud," No-Name was able to explain at last. "I had to walk. And the room was dark when I came in. I couldn't see anything." Everyone seemed to believe No-Name's reason for why he was so late. Even Karl believed it. After all, No-Name was very wet and covered with mud.

But then No-Name did something very strange. When no one else was looking, he winked at Karl. It was as if No-Name had pulled a joke on everyone but Karl. After that,

Karl didn't believe No-Name's story about the mud slide. He didn't believe it at all. In fact, he didn't know what to believe.

Lightning!

"Why was everyone standing over by the television when I came in?" No-Name asked. He was starting to look much better.

His words made everyone remember about the TV. Franco, Lola, Mark, and even Petra went over to have a close look at the haunted television. Karl was about to join them, but No-Name stopped him.

"Let's talk," he said in a whisper.

Karl was glad to have a private talk with No-Name. "OK," he said. "Do you want to start, or shall I?"

"Just tell me one thing," said No-Name. "Do you think Merl was murdered?"

Karl looked at the four people on the other side of the room. They had the back off the TV. Karl knew that they would probably not find any clues.

"Let's just say that I can see how someone *could* have murdered Merl. It's possible, at least."

"I knew it!"

"But that doesn't mean that he *was* murdered," Karl was quick to add. "Everything else has to fit together, too. There has to be a reason—a good reason—for someone to kill."

"We're not short of reasons," said No-Name. "Believe me, I could go down the line."

"Why don't you?"

"OK. We can start with Petra. She's crazy—that is, she *acts* crazy. But is she really crazy? She's seen a number of doctors since Merl died, but she's never been put away. As a matter of fact, Merl wanted her to see a doctor before he died. But she wouldn't. They had big fights about it all the time.

"Now to Franco—the world's best magician. He knew that as long as Merl was alive, he didn't have a chance to be number one. But with Merl out of the picture, it was easy for him to be the best. He knew all of Merl's tricks. He also had most of Merl's props. I tell you, Franco almost danced at Merl's wake.

"That brings us to Lola Nikel. She helped Merl on stage, you know. Her job was very important and she was very good at it—one of the best. But Merl didn't pay her much money.

And he had her under a very hard contract. The contract said she could never be a magician on her own or work for another magician as long as Merl was alive. And it said she couldn't work in any other part of show business as long as Merl was in show business. Lola turned down parts in a lot of movies because of her contract with Merl. She hated it. I've often heard her say that Merl was the reason she never became famous.

"And finally we come to Mark. He's the one, if you ask me. He had the best reason of all for killing Merl. He–"

No-Name stopped suddenly when a loud noise came from upstairs. The others in the room all rushed past Karl and No-Name on their way to the hall.

"What was it?" Lola asked.

"It sounded like a gun to me," said Mark.

"It came from upstairs," Franco said.

"Merl's room," said Petra. "It must have come from Merl's room."

By this time, the four of them were out the door. Karl heard the trick hall go off like a jack-in-the-box. Then everything was quiet again.

Karl was not as quick to rush out of the room

as the others. The sudden noise from upstairs had made him start thinking about the house. The house was very old; its walls were thick. It wasn't easy to tell just where a sound made in it came from.

No-Name was standing beside him. "I think we should follow them," he said, pointing to the hall.

Then one of the people upstairs screamed.

Lightning!

When Karl and No-Name got to Merl's room, Petra was standing in a corner screaming. Lola was stiff with shock. Both Franco and Mark were white as ghosts.

And no wonder. There was blood everywhere —fresh blood, bright red, warm to the touch. Most of the blood was on the top of Merl's bed. Some was on the rug around it.

"I think I'm going to be sick," said Franco. He ran out of the room. Lola followed him.

"Who is doing this—why?" shouted Mark.

Karl didn't like the sight of the blood any more than the others. But he walked right into the room and started looking around.

It was hard for him to think, however. Petra was screaming something about Merl's ghost.

Then, suddenly Mark took Petra's arm and the two rushed out of the room.

That left Karl and No-Name alone. Karl kept looking around, but No-Name seemed more interested in the people who had just left.

"I don't think we should waste much time up here," said No-Name. "We should be keeping a close watch on those four."

But Karl kept looking. He spoke to No-Name. "Down in the study you were telling me about Mark Steiner. Why don't you finish what you were saying?"

"OK. Mark took $1 million out of Merl's bank on a Friday. Merl died the next day. No one ever saw the money. Sure, Mark says Merl put the money in the safe that Friday night. But who knows if it's really there or not? We may never know."

Karl shook his head. He could find no clues in the bloody mess. Someone had done this just a few minutes ago. But who? And why?

Karl looked at No-Name. "By the way, I understand that you and Merl were fighting about something the night he died."

Suddenly, No-Name didn't seem so sure of himself. "Yes," he said. "Merl and I fought."

CHAPTER 9
BEGINNING OF THE END

"Merl was my brother," said No-Name. "None of the others knows this. I was the only one he ever really trusted. He told me everything. He even sent me all his plans and drawings for the Great Escape. I was the only one besides Merl who knew how he was planning to do that act. He asked me to burn all his papers if he should die. I did as he asked."

No-Name was quiet for a few seconds. Then he went on. "That's why I'm so sure that Merl didn't kill himself. He had been planning the Great Escape for years. And he was all set to go with it. It would have been better than Houdini's best. Merl would have gone down in history with that act."

"But what about your fight with him the night he died?" Karl wanted to know.

"That was nothing, really. We were fighting

about this 'returning from the dead' kick he was on. I thought it was silly, and I told him so. But Merl was sure he could do it. I said he was crazy, and one thing led to another. By the time the others got to the house, Merl and I were really shouting at each other."

"And that's all you were fighting about?"

"That's it. We used to fight like that all the time. Brothers are like that, you know. So what do you think, Mr. Baumer?"

Karl's head was spinning. The facts about this case were going around and around in his mind. He had learned too much, too soon, from too many.

And it was all *too* strange.

"I need a little more time to think," he said. "Perhaps we should get back down to the study."

"OK," said No-Name. "But do something for me, will you? When the time comes, point out the killer to everyone at once. And do it in the study–OK?"

"Sure, but–"

"Don't worry. I'll take care of the rest."

Karl wanted to ask what in the world No-Name was talking about. But things started happening fast, and Karl's thought was lost.

Lightning!

The lights went out. Shouts came from the first floor of the house. Karl and No-Name felt their way down the stairs and into the study as fast as they could.

The television set was on again. And once more it showed a picture of Merl the Magnificent. Only this time the picture moved. This time the picture of Merl slowly looked around the room. Then the TV went off, and the lights came back on.

Karl took a good, long look at the people in the study. Now would be the best time to speak up and solve this case, he thought. There is only one problem. I don't know who did it.

Then Karl realized that it didn't really matter who killed Merl. Karl knew *how* Merl was murdered, and that was most important. This murder is going to solve itself, Karl thought with a smile.

Karl walked over and threw a big log on the fire. Then he asked everyone to come over and sit by the fire, and they did. It was very quiet when Karl started to talk again.

"You should all know that I believe your

friend Merl the Magnificent was murdered. I am now ready to tell you how it was done and who did it."

Outside, the wind began to blow again. But inside, no one moved. The room was as quiet and still as death itself.

Karl went on. "Merl died sometime *before* everyone went upstairs to their rooms–not after. The shot you all heard later was to trick you. It was supposed to make you think that Merl had just killed himself, and it worked."

"How could Merl have died before then?" asked Mark. "We were all down here together after Merl went up to his room."

"Except that each of you left the room to knock on Merl's door at least once–remember? The killer probably walked right in without stopping to knock. He or she then used a gun with a silencer on it and shot Merl. Then the killer took the silencer off the gun and put the gun in Merl's hand."

"It could have been any one of us then," said Lola Nikel.

"That's right," said Karl. "Any one of you could have killed Merl. But only one of you could have pulled off the next part. It wasn't until later—after all of you were in your own rooms—that a shot was heard. Then the five of you rushed out into the hall to see what had happened. When Merl didn't come out, you all thought the shot must have come from his room. And when you found Merl's body, that seemed to prove it. No one ever thought that the shot could have come from some other room."

"Another room?" asked Franco. "How can that be?"

"The killer had two guns," said Karl. "One gun was used to kill Merl, and was then left with Merl's body. The killer fired the second gun later from his or her own room. This gun had blanks in it, of course. The killer then ran out into the hall like everyone else. And no one ever thought about it—until tonight."

"Hold it," said Mark. "Most of the rooms are right next to at least one other room. I think it would have been very easy for any of us to tell if a shot had been fired in the room next door."

"A good point," said Karl. "There are six rooms upstairs. Four of the rooms are at one end of the hall, two on each side. If the shot had been fired from one of those four rooms, someone would have been able to tell. But there is one room by itself, right across the hall from Merl's room. . . ."

"Just a minute," said Lola Nikel, standing. "That was my room."

Karl turned suddenly to face Lola. "Then you killed Merl. You were the only one who could have fired a gun in your room without getting caught. Come to think of it, you knew more about Merl's guns than anyone else."

"What you're saying is crazy," said Lola. "For one thing, you have no way to prove any of it. You can't even prove that Merl was murdered, much less who did it. You're just guessing. We went through all of this with the police 13 years ago. I don't see why we have to go through it again with you."

If she's guilty, Karl thought, she's playing it very cool. And besides that, she's right. I can't prove a thing I said.

CHAPTER 10
The Clock Strikes Nine

What happened next was like a dream.

First the television set came back on. Once again the picture it showed was Merl the Magnificent. This time Merl was looking right at Lola Nikel.

Then the lights went off. And the fire went out, too—just like that. Now the only light in the room came from the haunted television.

"Lola," a voice said. The voice was a loud whisper that didn't seem to come from the TV. In fact, it didn't seem to come from any one place. And yet it came from every place.

"Lola," it whispered. "Why? Tell me why."

Everyone in the room looked at Lola.

Lightning!

"Lola. . . ."

"Shut up!" Lola screamed suddenly. "You're

dead! You can't escape from death—no one can!"

"Lola. . . ."

"This can't be happening," Lola yelled. She was really shouting now. She moved across the room. But the picture moved, too. It followed her with its eyes.

". . . Tell me, Lola. . . ."

"No! You're dead! My life is my own now." Lola covered her ears with her hands, but it didn't seem to do her any good.

"Why couldn't you have waited, Lola? My Great Escape was just two days away."

The words seemed to drive Lola mad. She picked up the first thing she saw—a small lamp. "Your Great Escape!" she said. "That's all you ever thought about, Merl. I hated that! I hated you! I would kill you again if I could!"

With that said, Lola threw the lamp at the television. A crash followed, and the set was broken.

Then the lights came on. And a voice much like the TV voice said, "OK, Lola. That's all we need." It was No-Name. And he was pointing a gun at Lola.

"We've recorded everything you've said and done. We can play it back on any television set at any time."

Karl moved to Lola. Her arms hung at her sides, and she looked straight ahead. Karl took out his handcuffs and put them on her. She made no trouble.

Mark, Franco, and Petra all talked at once.

"That picture we saw on TV—was that Merl?"

"No," said No-Name. "It was a man made up to look like Merl."

"What about the rest of it—the blood, the lights going off and on?"

"All the work of my people. There are about 20 of us. We have a special effects lab set up in the empty house next door. But you almost stopped the show when you took the back off the TV. One of our women fixed it while we were all upstairs. Then Merl had his grand finale after all."

Now it was Franco's turn to ask a question. "Are you and your people with the police, No-Name?"

No-Name smiled for the first time. "In a way, I suppose. At least some of the time. Let's just say that we often do special work for the police. But we did all of this on our own."

"You're quite a magician yourself, No-Name," said Karl.

No-Name turned to Karl. "Well, we couldn't have done it without you, Mr. Baumer. I've known for years that Merl was murdered. But I never knew who did it or how it was done. You, on the other hand, worked it all out in just a few hours. I should have called on you years ago."

The police came to the door. They had been called by one of No-Name's people. A few minutes later, Lola was gone.

After that, everyone began getting ready to leave. Then yet another strange thing happened. A big old clock in the study began to ring out, like it was sounding the hour.

Petra ran over to the clock and stood in front of it. Mark and Franco and No-Name stared.

"What's going on?" asked Karl. "Why is everyone acting so surprised?"

"Because that clock hasn't worked since the night Merl died," No-Name said.

"Funny it should start now," Franco said.

When the clock finished ringing, Petra turned to the others. She was laughing and jumping up and down like a child. "It rang nine times," she said. "Did you hear? Don't you see? It rang *nine times*!"

Karl, Mark, Franco and No-Name looked at one another. None of them seemed to have any idea what Petra was talking about.

Half an hour later, Karl drove through

Frankfurt in his rented Volkswagen bus. He was on his way home after a long, hard night.

The rain was over, and the sky had cleared. Karl could see the Bad Moon. It was going down. Soon it would be gone. But there was no telling when it would be back.

As he drove, Karl couldn't help thinking about Petra. She seemed so crazy. Yet she was the only one who had realized what was happening with that old clock. She was the only one who had kept track of how many times the clock rang.

And she was the only one who had thought to use that number to open Merl's safe.